The BEST Thing About
Easter

by Christine Harder Tangvald

**What is Easter really about?
Look inside and let's find out!**

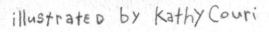

illustrated by Kathy Couri

First Paperback Printing, 1997
The Standard Publishing Company, Cincinnati, Ohio.
A division of Standex International Corporation.
Text © 1993 by Christine Harder Tangvald.
Illustrations © 1993 The Standard Publishing Company.
All rights reserved. Printed in the United States of America.

04 03 02 01 00 99 98 97   5 4 3 2 1

Library of Congress Catalog Card Number 92-32823. ISBN 0-7847-0578-X.

Scripture verses adapted from *The Bible in Today's English Version*.
© 1966,1971, 1976, by the American Bible Society. Used by permission.

Do you like Easter?
I DO! I think Easter is FUN!

I like to dye Easter eggs
all different colors —

Pink **ones,** and Green **ones,**
and Blue **ones,** **and**

Orange **ones, and**

yellow **ones.**

Which one is
    YOUR favorite?

THEN . . .
After we dye the eggs,

... we HIDE them!

I love to hunt for
Easter eggs, don't you?

Here's one, right here!

How many can you find?

Yes, I think Easter eggs are Fun!

But Easter eggs aren't the BEST thing about Easter!

Sometimes we have CANDY Easter eggs with soft, squishy marshmallow on the inside.

Yum,

Yum!

yum,

Sometimes we have gooey, chewy jelly beans that taste like lemon or cherry or peppermint!

Yum, yum, yum!

And sometimes we have dark chocolate Easter bunnies that melt in your mouth!

Yum,

Yum,

Yum!

I like Easter candy . . . A LOT!

But candy isn't the BEST thing about Easter.

Did you ever pet a soft, furry bunny at Easter time?

I did — at my uncle's farm.

Pet, Pet, Pet. Pat, Pat, Pat.

I like soft, furry bunnies.

Once my cousin got a fuzzy yellow duck that said,

Quack! Quack! Quack!

My other cousin got a cute
baby chick that said,

I like furry bunnies and fuzzy
ducks and cute baby chicks,
don't you?

But bunnies and ducks
and chicks aren't the BEST
thing about Easter.

**Easter is in the springtime,
and guess what happens THEN!**

I Run,

Run

Run

**on the
green, green grass,
UP the hill and DOWN the hill
in the bright, warm sunshine.**

WHEE !!

Just WATCH me!

Everything is Bursting

with new life in the springtime.

But springtime isn't the BEST thing about Easter, either.

I like to get ALL DRESSED UP on Easter Sunday, don't you?

First I scrub, scrub, scrub in the tub and get all clean.

Then I Brush, Brush, Brush my hair.

**And then I put on my
VERY BEST CLOTHES!**

Then at church on Easter Sunday,

we Talk
and Laugh
together,

we Sit and Sing together,

and

we listen and Pray together.

We have a treat together too.

Oh, YES! I like getting all dressed up and being together on Easter Sunday.

But even that isn't the BEST thing about Easter.

The very BEST THING about Easter is . . .

. . . JESUS . . .
God's own Son!

Oh, yes! JESUS **is the**
BEST THING about Easter.

You see, we have
Easter because of

JeSuS.

Easter is about
something wonderful
that was part of God's
AMAZING plan.

First a very sad
thing happened.

Jesus died on
the cross.

But guess what!

Jesus Did Not Stay Dead!

No, He Did Not!

On the very first Easter morning, God made Jesus ALIVE again! The tomb was EMPTY!

Jesus' friends were SO **surprised**

and So **happy to see him again.**

"Jesus is Alive!" **they said.**
"He is really alive!"

And then, a little later,
do you know what God did?

He took Jesus

up, up, up...

**right
through
a cloud into**

HEAVEN!

**It was all
part of
GOD'S
amazing
plan!**

But the MOST amazing part of God's plan is that Jesus died and Lives Again... **for ME!**

It's TRUE! Because Jesus loves Me, **you see.**

He loves YOU **too.**

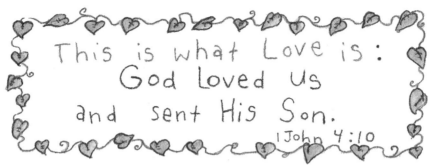

This is what Love is:
God loved us
and sent His Son.

1 John 4:10

**Oh yes!
I like Easter eggs, and
I like Easter candy, and
I like soft furry bunnies and
     fuzzy baby ducks, and
I like getting all dressed up
     and being together on
     Easter Sunday.**

But...

. . . the BEST THING about Easter is

Jesus!

I'm GLAD Jesus loves ME!

I'm really, REALLY glad, aren't you?

Happy Easter, Everyone!